Catnapped!

W9-BEG-346

PUPPY PIRATES

Catnapped!

by Erin Soderberg
illustrations by Russ Cox

SCHOLASTIC INC.

For sweet, smart, silly Ruby
—E.S.

ISBN 978-1-338-04846-9

12 11 10 9 8 7 6 5 4   17 18 19 20 21

Printed in the U.S.A.   40

First Scholastic printing, April 2016

CONTENTS

Catnipped

Wally's tail wagged at the sight of a soft, sweet mouse. His nose twitched. The gentle golden retriever slowed to a walk. He crept quietly over the wooden planks of the fishing pier. Closer . . . closer . . .

He pounced. "Gotcha!"

The mouse darted out of his grasp. Wally leaped on it again. This time, he caught it! The little critter stayed very, very still. Wally patted it with his paw and looked up. His two pug friends,

1

Piggly and Puggly, were watching him closely.

Wally poked the mouse with his nose. *Squeak!* The mouse smelled funny. It didn't smell like fur or dirt or hay, like all the other mice Wally had chased. It also didn't smell like one of the filthy rats that lived on the puppy pirate ship. Wally pushed the little mouse with his paw again.

The pug twins burst out laughing.

Wally's best friend, a boy named Henry, leaned toward Wally. "In case you were wondering, mate? That's a fake mouse. I think the pugs are playing pranks again."

"Aw, Wally," said Piggly. Her gold tooth glimmered in the early-morning sun. "We didn't mean to trick you."

Puggly wagged her tail. It was the puppy pirates' big day out in town, and the fancy pug was dressed in her favorite outfit—purple booties, a black velvet cap with a tall feather, and a fine golden cape. She sat primly and explained, "We're practicing our prank for the kitten pirates."

"This one is a classic," Piggly snorted. "We call it Catnipped Kitty. Have you ever seen a kitty with a nose full of catnip, mates?" She winked at the small group of puppy pirates who had gathered around.

Wally shook his head. He didn't know much about cats. He knew they hated water, had sharp claws, and were very stuck-up. (That's what the pugs had told him, anyway.) He also knew that the kitten pirates were the puppy pirates' worst enemies.

A bulldog named Spike whined, "Kitten pirates? Where?" The nervous bulldog looked like one of the toughest dogs on the puppy pirate crew. He could out-tug anyone if he wanted to. But he never did. Spike was a scaredy-dog.

"Look over there," Piggly said. She cocked her head in the direction of a pirate ship anchored far out in the harbor. "There's the kitten ship. It's called the *Nine Lives*."

The puppy pirate ship—the *Salty Bone*—was docked in town for the day. The puppy pirates needed to load up with supplies. The crew had a few hours off to run and play and explore before they set sail again.

Puggly winked. "That boatful of no-fun furballs is gonna be hanging out in town today, too. Which makes this the *purr*-fect day for pranks!"

A warning growl came from behind Wally. It was Old Salt, the oldest and wisest member of the puppy pirate crew. "Remember," the peglegged Bernese mountain dog said, "we have a truce with the kitten pirates when we both sail into town. They leave us alone, and we leave them alone. Don't go lookin' for trouble."

The younger pups nodded.

"We don't need any of your monkey business," Old Salt said.

"No monkey business," Piggly promised.

As soon as Old Salt hobbled away, Puggly snorted, "Aye. Just a little kitty business."

"Here come the kitten pirates," Henry said, pointing.

A pair of blue-eyed Siamese kittens pranced toward them, tails held high.

"Here, kitty, kitty!" Piggly giggled. "I said, *heeeere,* kitty, kitties." She nudged her twin sister.

Puggly trotted down the fishing pier, swishing her curly tail back and forth. Now Wally saw that a piece of string was tied to Puggly's tail. The small stuffed mouse was at the end of the string. When Puggly wagged her tail, the little mouse bumped and thumped along after her. It looked and sounded just like a real mouse wiggling down the pier.

Swish!

Squeak!

Wiggle!

Piggly was laughing so hard she began to sneeze.

The two Siamese kittens hissed, "Ahoy, ya scurrrrvy dogs."

The pups growled back.

"Remember what Old Salt said," Wally whispered nervously. "We don't want any trouble."

"Trouble?" squeaked Spike. The fat bulldog dashed behind Wally. "Nope. We don't need trouble. No, sirree."

Piggly snorted, "Eh, they're just cats. How much trouble could a few furry felines be?"

Puggly wagged her tail harder. The stuffed

mouse flopped and squeaked on the wooden dock. Suddenly, the cats spotted it.

"Just wait, Wally," Piggly said, nudging him. "Watch and learn."

Wally hid his nose between his paws and peeked up at the kittens.

The kitten pirates crept toward the mouse. Their noses twitched. They arched their backs, popped their claws, and leaped.

Pounce!

Scaredy-Dogs

The Siamese kittens dove on the mouse. They chewed and tugged at the soft toy, pulling it off its string. They rubbed and rolled against it, then batted it into the air. They squealed and squeaked and flopped all over the wooden dock. They were totally out of control!

Wally had never seen anything like it before.

Piggly and Puggly roared with laughter. "There's catnip in the mice," Puggly explained.

"The stuff makes cats crazy. Even the boring ones."

The other puppy pirates crowded around to watch the kittens going wild. Even Spike crept close enough to see what was going on.

Both kittens screeched when they knocked over a bucket. The bucket tipped. Water flew

everywhere. Dozens of lobsters skittered out and down the pier. Spike yelped and hid behind Henry. But the cats ignored the lobsters' clacking claws. They were too busy fighting over the stuffed mouse.

Wally knew cats hated water, but these cats barely seemed to notice that they were wet.

They bounced and tumbled in the puddle, then chased the toy farther down the dock. Their fur was soaked and matted with dirt.

"Will the catnip hurt them?" Wally asked Puggly.

"Nah," said Puggly. "Makes cats act funny. But once we take away the mice, they will be back to normal. Just embarrassed, is all."

The kittens' tongues lolled out of their mouths. As they wrestled, they rolled closer and closer to the edge of the pier. *What if they fall off?* Wally shuddered at the thought. *What if that was me? What if I was wearing the kittens' claws?* The ocean was cold and deep and wet. Wally would want someone to help him.

And he definitely wouldn't want to look so silly in front of all these other pirates.

"In case you were wondering?" Henry said, his eyebrows shooting up. "Cats are proud animals. They hate to be embarrassed like this."

Spike whispered, "I wish someone would take the mouse away from them."

Wally agreed with Henry and Spike. The pugs' prank had lasted long enough. If Old Salt were there, he would put an end to it.

But Old Salt wasn't there. Which meant someone else had to do it.

"Avast!" Wally said suddenly, surprising even himself.

"Eh?" barked Piggly.

Wally leaped onto the mouse. He ripped it out of the cats' claws and tossed the mouse toward the water. The kittens chased after it but stopped when the toy plopped into the ocean far below. Exhausted, both Siamese kittens collapsed onto the dock. Within seconds, they were fast asleep.

Wally tucked his tail between his legs. He could feel the pugs staring at him. Were they mad he had ruined their prank?

"Takes a mighty brave pirate to stick up for a cat," Puggly said finally. She didn't seem angry at all. She waddled down the pier, and a few paces away, she turned back to Wally. "You coming, Wally? We best be getting to the dog park to meet the rest of the crew."

"Aye!" Wally barked happily.

As he strutted through the crowds with Henry, Spike, Piggly, and Puggly, Wally could feel the town dogs' eyes on him and his mates. He walked tall and proud, showing off his pirate bandanna.

They passed through the market, gazing at all the carts and tables heaped with food. Steak-Eye, the ship's cook, was in a back alley arguing with a pup outside the butcher shop. As the feisty Chihuahua shouted and stomped, his tail whacked to and fro. Bones and a basket of dog treats toppled to the ground. "No, I will *not* take scraps!" Steak-Eye yipped. "Top-choice meat only. I buy the best for me crew."

The butcher pup looked nervous. He offered a piece of crispy bacon to Steak-Eye to apologize. Wally laughed. Steak-Eye seemed scary, but the ship's cook was all bark and no bite.

Just past the market, Wally spotted the ship's first mate. "Curly!" The tough miniature poodle was slinking along the edge of a pink building. It looked like she was trying to hide. "Curly!" he shouted again. "The dog park is this way."

Curly ignored him and ducked inside the shop.

"Pampered Pooch?" Henry said, reading the sign on the door. He wrinkled his nose. "Why is she going in there?"

"Curly gets a trim and a perm every time we get shore leave. You think hair like that just does itself?" Puggly sniffed. "Me? I wake up like this. I'm what's called a natural beauty."

At the edge of the shops, the friends came to a large dog park. In the center of the park was a small clear pond. Many of the puppy pirates were splashing around in the deep water. It was hard to swim in the ocean because of the waves. But here on land, the dogs loved to swim and play.

All except Wally.

"Come on in, Walty!" Captain Red Beard barked.

Henry tossed a ball into the pond for Wally. But Wally didn't move. "What's wrong, mate?" Henry asked.

Wally didn't answer. This was the moment he had been dreading since he first joined the pirate crew. After all, what kind of puppy pirate is afraid to swim?

Back when he had been a bitty pup, Wally had fallen into a lake near the farm. When he

yelped for help, he got a mouthful of water and panicked. Somehow he had managed to paddle to shore. But as soon as Wally's paws had touched land, he began to shake with fear.

He had never tried to swim again. He was afraid.

17

Spike was chewing a stick nearby. He lifted his meaty head and whispered to Wally, "Scared of water, are ya? I get it, mate. There's nothing scarier than swimming. Except cats . . . and chickens . . . and bilge rats . . . and Steak-Eye . . . and grass that touches my belly . . . and those little snails that sometimes get stuck to the side of our ship . . . and . . ."

Wally didn't want to be a scaredy-dog like Spike. But he didn't want to tell a fib, either. So instead of explaining why he wasn't swimming, he stretched out against Henry's leg and took a nap.

Before long, the puppy pirate crew was joined by a group of town dogs eager to hear stories of pirate adventures. Everyone climbed out of the pond and shook off. The town dogs curled up in a pile, listening as Captain Red Beard told tall tales of life on the high seas.

"And then there was the time we found a

gazillion gold coins and *then* fought off six hundred cats plus the Sea Slug, all in one afternoon!"

"Not all in one day?" gasped a Labrador retriever.

"Absolushy!" Red Beard boasted, holding up a paw. "That means *yep* in . . . um, Piratish. Piratish language. We pirates speak a bazillion languages, y'know."

The rest of the puppy pirates snickered. Captain Red Beard had a habit of stretching the truth and making up words. The scraggly terrier captain gave his crew a look that said, *Quiet!* The puppy pirates all stopped laughing at once. But in the silence that followed, something else began to laugh.

Many somethings.

The dogs looked around. Where was the sound coming from?

Spike was the first to howl. "Kitten pirates! Everybody run!"

Cat-Attack

It was an ambush! The entire kitten crew was crawling over the hillside. The cats were clearly angry, all hisses and claws. The town pups ran off, but the puppy pirates prepared for a fight.

Most of the puppy pirates, anyway. Not Spike. He just roamed in circles, shaking with terror. "What do we do? What do we *do-oooo-ooooo*?"

Captain Red Beard pushed to the front of

his crew. He went nose to nose with the kitten captain. "We had a deal, Captain Lucinda the Loud! We no attacky you, you no attacky us."

Lucinda the Loud hissed. "We *had* a deal . . . until your pugs broke the rules. Bad dogs! You should know better than to play catnip pranks on Moopsy and Boopsy."

"Uh-oh," Piggly squeaked. She and Puggly quickly backed away from the face-off. They ducked beneath a leafy bush.

"Moopsy and Boopsy?" Puggly snorted, once they were safely out of sight. She tried to hide her giggles inside her cape. "The Siamese cats are named *Moopsy* and *Boopsy*?" Laughing and sneezing, she poked her sister. "Piggly, come with me. I've got an idea!"

No one but Wally noticed the pugs sneak away. All eyes were on the two pirate captains.

"You're outnumbered!" Lucinda the Loud

21

yelled. "You have no choice but to surrender."

"Never!" Red Beard barked. "Puppy pirates, prepare for battle!"

Lucinda the Loud was right: the puppies *were* outnumbered. They were also tired from a morning of playing in the pond. They had no energy left for a fight. But they had no other choice.

Hisssss!

Cats and dogs jumped at the strange sound. Little black spigots poked out of the grass all over the dog park. Then water came shooting out!

"Me fur!" Lucinda the Loud shrieked, trying to shield herself. The kitten pirates panicked and ran toward the trees for cover.

"En garde!" Puggly said, whipping her cape in the air. "Pugs to the rescue!"

Piggly cheered. "The best part of this park is a sprinkler system for hot days—and for cat attack-ack-ack-acks!"

Red Beard howled. The rest of the crew joined in. "Flee, kitty cats, flee!" he barked joyfully. Even Lucinda the Loud was cowering under a leafy tree. "Neener-nanner-noo-noo!" Red Beard teased. "The puppy pirates win again! Now, pups, to the ship. With paste!"

23

Curly said, "I think you mean *haste,* Captain Red Beard? Move fast, yes?"

"As I said: to the ship, with pasty haste!" The captain raced through the park, with the rest of the crew hot on his tail. The sprinklers couldn't stay on forever.

Wally stopped when he realized Spike wasn't with them. The bulldog was frozen in place near the pond, staring at a tiny kitten. She was perched on a branch, giving him the stink eye. "C'mon, Spike," Wally said, tugging his collar. "We need to get out of here before the sprinklers shut off."

Nearby, Piggly and Puggly were helping Steak-Eye and Old Salt drag the cook's big bag of steaks. The pugs urged the other two to go on ahead. "It's me and Puggly's fault we're in this mess," Piggly said. "We can get Henry to help us carry the steaks."

Steak-Eye squinted his bulgy eyes. "Fine. But

don't go stealin' me food, Piggly. I know *exactly* how many steaks the butcher put in that bag."

"Yeah, yeah," grumbled Piggly. Old Salt and Steak-Eye ran ahead. Piggly, Puggly, and Henry tugged at the bag of meat.

Wally and Spike caught up to them. Wally was trying to keep the scared bulldog calm. "Deep breaths, Spike. Let your tongue flap out. There you go."

Between the weight of the steaks and Spike's slow, shaky legs, the group of five soon fell far behind the rest of the crew. The cats glared at them from hiding spots in the trees. The water kept raining down.

"Do you hear something?" Piggly said, stopping abruptly. The others froze beside her.

"Something? What something?" Spike curled into a tight ball.

Then Wally heard it, too. A faint *woof* coming from above.

"Is there a *dog* in that tree?" Wally asked, confused. How could a pup climb a tree?

"Woof, woof, help me!" came a tiny voice from way up in the branches.

Henry, Wally, Puggly, and even Spike all rushed toward the tree. Only Piggly stayed where she was. "Is it just me, or does that sound a lot like—"

Plop! A net fell from the tree, right on top of Wally, Henry, Spike, and Puggly.

"—like a cat," Piggly finished.

Moopsy and Boopsy, the two Siamese cats, poked their heads out of the leafy branches high above the pups. "Ha-*ha!*" the two cats cheered together. "Now who's laughing, pugs?"

"You missed *me,* hair balls," Piggly taunted.

Wally barked, "Piggly, go for help! Run while you can."

Spike wailed, "Tell the others we've— we've—we've been *catnapped!*"

The Brig Jig

Wally, Henry, Puggly, and Spike were prisoners on the kitten ship.

"In case you were wondering, mates?" Henry said. He sat on the floor with his back against a cold, damp wall. Gently, he twisted the soft fur under Wally's chin. "This is not looking so good."

"Not looking good," Spike whimpered, closing his eyes. "Not looking good, not looking good, not looking—"

"Calm down, will you?" Puggly said primly. "So we're prisoners on the kitten ship. What's the big deal?"

"What's the big deal?" Spike howled. "They're *cats!*"

Moopsy and Boopsy had waited until the park sprinklers turned off. Then they leashed up their prisoners—even Henry—and led them out of the park. They were all long gone before Piggly could bring help.

The sneaky cats had pulled their prisoners down a dark alley, loaded them onto a dinghy, and locked them in the stinky brig at the bottom of the *Nine Lives*. The kitten pirates had also stolen Steak-Eye's bag of meat. Wally hadn't yet decided which was worse: being catnapped, or having to tell Steak-Eye they had lost his juicy steaks.

The brig was small, and the kitten ship

smelled like tuna and hair balls. *Cat* hair balls.
The combination of the tight space and the smell
was driving Spike crazy. He dashed around the
tiny cell, his feet flying in all directions. Then he

30

pawed at the metal bars, trying to climb them.

Puggly watched the chubby bulldog curiously. "He's doin' a brig jig," she said, giggling.

"What's a brig jig?" Wally asked.

Puggly sneezed. "I made it up. It looks like Spike's trying to dance his way out of jail. Dancin' a jig in the brig. *Brig jig.*" Puggly waited for someone to laugh, but no one was in much of a laughing mood. Finally, she whispered, "*Piggly* would think it's funny."

When he got tired of climbing the walls, Spike tried digging a hole in the solid floor below their feet. When that didn't work, either, he began to wail. Big, sad sobs that echoed around them.

"Piggly went for help, Spike," Wally reminded him. "I'm sure our crew is just trying to come up with a plan for how to sneak on board to steal us back."

The *Nine Lives* rocked and swayed. It lurched. Spike, who was now curled into a chubby ball, began to roll around the floor like a giant bug.

"In case you were wondering?" Henry said quietly. "The ship's moving."

"Moving?" Spike shot up and ran in circles. "If we be moving, Captain Red Beard and the others are never going to get to us! Never!"

"Silence!" Lucinda the Loud hissed. No one had heard her coming. The longhaired kitten captain stood in shadow nearby, her fluffy tail swishing silently. A smaller tabby cat stood at her side. The two Siamese kittens paced nearby, grinning.

Spike tried hiding under Wally. But he was far too big to fit.

"Allow me to introduce myself!" Lucinda the Loud boomed. "I am Lucinda the Loud, the captain of the kitten pirates." Her fierce green

eyes focused on Henry. "And you ... are the funniest-looking dog I have ever seen."

Wally stepped forward and said, "Henry's a boy, ma'am. My best mate, and one of the finest pirates in all the world."

"I do not know this breed you call boy!" shouted Lucinda the Loud.

The tabby cat whispered something in her ear.

Lucinda boomed, "Speak up, Fluffy!"

The cat called Fluffy sighed. "It's Fluffy the Claw. *The Claw!* If you insist on calling yourself Lucinda the Loud, please call me the Claw. Skip the Fluffy part, please." The tabby cat shook his head. "And, Captain, a boy is not a breed of dog. It's a human."

"Ah, yes!" shouted Lucinda the Loud. "I see, Fluffy. A human dog. *Human-dog. Hu-dog.* For short, I shall call it a *hog!*" She stared at Henry for another minute, then continued, "Now, in case it is not clear: you are our prisoners. We have sent a message in a bottle to your captain. If he wants to get his pups and his hog back again, he must turn over his jewels and maps. And your softest beds. All the best loot."

34

"Not my bed!" Spike cried.

Puggly growled. "You can't do this."

"Ah!" meowed Lucinda the Loud. "I already have. The message went doodly-doodly-doo, floating all across the waves. Your ship got our message. The puppy pirate crew has until tomorrow to give us their loot. Or we'll show you what kitten pirates do with dogs." She turned to Fluffy. "I forget, what exactly do we do with dogs?"

Fluffy whispered something in her ear.

Lucinda screeched, "You know I can't hear you when you whisper, Fluffy!"

The kitten pirate captain turned and pranced out of the brig. Fluffy followed. The Siamese cats giggled and slunk after them. They winked at the prisoners just before the door slammed shut.

The puppy pirates were alone again. Trapped.

Wally stood and turned to his friends. "We can't let Captain Red Beard get bossed around by a bunch of *cats*!"

"How are we supposed to stop them?" Spike asked in a shaky voice.

"I hate to admit it, but Spike's got a point," said Puggly.

"In case you were wondering, I don't think our crew can help us now," Henry said.

Wally took a deep breath. "Henry's right. That's why ..." He looked long and hard at Spike, Puggly, and Henry. "Mates, we are going to rescue ourselves!"

The Brains of the Boat

A moment later, Fluffy the Claw stepped softly back into the room. "Ahoy," the quiet tabby cat purred.

None of the puppy pirates said anything.

"What do you want, *Fluffy*?" Puggly finally grumbled. "Shouldn't you be busy taking a cat-nap or licking your fur or something?"

The small tabby spoke softly. "As the ship's first mate, I wanted to offer my apology." Even

Spike perked up a bit when he heard that. "And you may call me the Claw. Skip the Fluffy, if you please."

"Does your captain know you're here?" Wally asked.

"Captain Lucinda the Loud doesn't know much," said the Claw. Then he looked sorry he'd said it out loud. "Let's keep that a secret between us."

Puggly laughed. "Sounds a lot like a captain we know." She cocked her head at the tabby cat. "Are you like our first mate, Curly, then? The brains of the boat?"

"You could say that, yes," the Claw purred. "My noble captain and I do not agree on everything. Today, we do not agree about what to do with you, our prisoners. I would like to set sail for the South Seas, on our next adventure. But my captain wants to play this silly game of cat and mouse with your ship. I think this is a waste of our time."

"We agree!" barked Wally. "Maybe if you just let us out of here, we could both be on our way."

The Claw paced back and forth, his tail flipping to and fro. On the end of his tail was a ring with a key. He dangled it in front of the prison bars. It was almost close enough to touch. "Perhaps I should do just that. . . ."

"Please, Fluffy. *The Claw*, sir," Wally said, feeling a tiny spark of hope. "Think of the wonderful adventures waiting for you in the South Seas. We were just there, and it was so nice."

"Very pretty," Spike offered.

"It's beautiful this time of year," Puggly added.

The Claw lifted his paw and licked it. "Even if I were to let you out of here, you'd still be trapped on the ship. How would you—" He cut himself off as the door flew open. A matted orange cat leaped into the room and yelled, "Fluffy, there's trouble above deck. Catnip!"

The Claw swung around and glared at the orange cat. "It's *the Claw*! And *how,* exactly, did catnip land on our ship?"

The orange cat looked scared. "Uh, Moopsy and Boopsy brought a whole crate of catnip-filled toys on board. I don't know what those two naughty kittens were planning to do with them."

"Where's the crate now?" the Claw hissed.

"I got it away from the twins," said the orange cat. "It's right out there."

"In the hallway?" the Claw meowed. "Where anyone could find it? If the rest of the crew gets hold of those toys, they will all leave their posts! Our whole ship will be chaos!"

"What should we do?" the orange cat asked.

The Claw went still as a statue, thinking. Finally, he said, "I'll hide the crate in the galley. No one but Hook the Cook goes in there, and he can't see or smell anything. Besides, the stink of his cookin' will mask the scent of catnip. As soon as we dock again, those toys are going heave-ho!"

"Aye, aye, Fluffy!" said the orange cat. "Uh, I mean, the Claw."

"Wait!" Wally yipped as the Claw and the orange cat turned to leave. "Don't forget about—" The kittens rushed out. The door slammed behind them. "Us."

"Nooooooo!" Spike moaned. "We were so close to getting out of here. *This* close." He held his paws together. "This . . ." *Sob.* "Close." *Snuffle.*

"It's okay," Wally said. He sounded more

42

confident than he felt. "We're gonna find some way out of here. I'm sure of it!"

"Does that mean you have an idea?" Puggly said hopefully.

Wally hung his head. "Not yet."

"In case you were wondering, mates? I have good news," Henry said. "Who wants to get back to the *Salty Bone?*"

"Maybe you should remind your boy that we're locked in," Puggly snorted. "Fluffy just hightailed it out of here without unlocking our cell."

Henry held out a fist. He opened his fingers. Something small and golden gleamed in his palm.

Spike danced his brig jig. "We're freeeeeee!"

Wally woofed, "Is that what I think it is?"

It was. Henry had the key. "Cats may be sneaky, but I'm sneakier," he said, grinning.

"That tabby cat didn't even notice when I reached right through the bars and grabbed the key off his tail. Only one thing to do now." He twisted the key in the lock, and something clicked. The door of their jail cell swung open. Henry waved his hand toward Puggly and said, "Ladies first."

6

The Digging Room

They marched out of the open cell door. Everyone's spirits were lifted. But outside the brig, all four of them stopped. They glanced left, then right. The puppy pirates weren't locked up anymore. But they were still lost on an enemy ship in the middle of the ocean—surrounded by kittens.

Spike whimpered. "What now?"

"Maybe we could try to swim away?" Puggly suggested.

Wally gulped. No way would he swim in the

ocean. There was nothing safe about that. But before he had to say it, Henry blurted out, "In case you were wondering, the best way to escape a pirate ship is to hop in a dinghy."

"Aye! Let's get above deck and find a dinghy. We can row home," Wally said happily. He loved dinghies. They were the little wooden boats that hung off the side of the ship. Just that morning, Henry had rowed one from the *Salty Bone* to shore. Morning seemed like a *very* long time ago now.

Henry rubbed his chin and added, "We have to remember, mates: the most important rule of being a prisoner on an enemy ship is to remain calm. Even if the cats are on our tail, we can't let them scare us!"

Wally woofed his agreement. "Aye!"

Puggly flapped her cape and growled, "They can't scare me."

"Nope, no thanks, not going to happen." Spike backed into a corner. "I'll just stay in the brig, if that's okay?"

"Spike," grumbled Puggly, "didn't you hear what the boy said? We need to remain calm and *not* let them scare us."

"Uh-huh," Spike whimpered. "Calm ... cats . . . no scare . . . no fear." He started shaking his head, hard. "No *way*! These are *kittens* you're talking about! They're fierce beasts."

Puggly giggled. "Aw, they're just a bunch of pussycats. Your paw's bigger than ol' Fluffy's head."

Wally stood before the big bulldog. "And remember: we're your crew, Spike. You can trust us, can't you? We'll get you out of here safely."

"You promise?" Spike asked in a tiny voice.

Wally couldn't promise—because he *wasn't* sure. But he was sure they couldn't leave Spike behind. And they couldn't stay in the brig forever. "I promise to try my best," said Wally. "We all will. We'll be back on board the *Salty Bone* in no time. You'll see. We can do it."

They all held their breath, waiting to see if Spike would go for it. Spike sighed. Then he heaved himself off the floor and said, "Okay, mates. I'm in."

Together, the prisoners tiptoed through the enemy ship. They poked their noses into dark hallways and small rooms, trying to find their way above deck.

The floors on the *Nine Lives* were made of wood, just like on the *Salty Bone*, but they were not nearly as scratched up. Tiny bells and stuffed mice hung from the ceilings. The walls were covered with a rough carpet that looked like it had done battle with hundreds of cat claws.

Unlike the *Salty Bone*, which had wide hallways, open spaces, and large rooms, the kitten ship was a maze of tight spaces and little cubbies. Every hall had many other corridors leading off of it. Most of the cabins were small and squeezy, just big enough for one or two cats to curl up in. There were rooms stacked on top of rooms. Henry had to duck and crawl in many spots to make it through.

Finally, a winding hallway dead-ended in a large cabin. Its door was unlocked. "No one in here," Puggly said, poking her snout inside. "But it sure smells pretty. Like roses and perfume and a warm spring day."

"The whole room is filled with sand!" Spike cried. Forgetting his fear, the big bulldog rushed through the doorway and into the room. "Mates! Lookie. The cats have a digging room. We need a digging room. How great would it be if we had a digging room?" He quickly set to work making a giant hole in the center of the sand.

Meanwhile, Puggly sniffed around the edges

of the room. "I'm trying to find what smells so pretty. I think they're hiding something pug-glorious in here! If it be jewels, I'll find it!"

Henry looked amused. "Um, mates? In case you were wondering, this is the cats' litter box. It's where they, uh . . . do their business."

"Pay bills and stuff?" asked Spike. He curled up to rest in his hole in the sand.

Henry's face turned red as he went on.

"Okay, so you don't seem to get that, do you? Let me say it like this. . . . You know how dogs like to go on trees? Well, cats like to go in sand. Sand just like this."

"This sand is their potty?" Spike shrieked. He scurried up and shook off. "Cats. Pee. In. This. Sand?"

"Shiver me timbers, they sure do make it smell beautiful," said Puggly. She hustled back out to the corridor. "Ah, well. Moving on!"

But no matter which direction they turned, they couldn't find their way up to the deck. It felt like they had been searching forever when they heard the *click-clack* of tiny claws against the wooden floor right around a corner. Someone was coming!

The puppies froze.

"What do you think the captain will do to the puppy pirate prisoners when she finds them?" a soft voice purred.

51

"The same thing she'll do to us if we *don't* find them," another voice answered.

"In case you were wondering?" Henry whispered. "I think now might be a good time to hide."

They moved very quickly but *very* quietly. Moments later, the four friends slipped through an unlocked door farther down the hallway. Henry eased the door closed behind them. Wally wagged his tail. Spike trembled in relief.

"Safe," Puggly said. "For now."

They turned around, and their eyes went wide.

A human girl glared back at them. "What, exactly, do you think you're doing in my cabin?"

Prove Yourself a Pirate

"You're a girl," Henry said. "What are you doing on a kitten ship?"

"You're a *boy*," she pointed out. A tiny gray kitten peeked out from under the girl's blanket and blinked sleepily at the intruders. "What are *you* doing on a kitten ship? With a bunch of"— she glanced at Wally, Puggly, and Spike— "dogs? And whatever you call that little wrinkled creature wearing a scarf?"

53

"I'm a pug, lady," snarled Puggly. "And this here is me cape!"

They could hear the muffled sound of cat paws padding past on the other side of the door. Henry put his finger to his lips and whispered, "Listen, we've been catnapped. The kittens on this ship are after us. Please, can we just hang out in here until the coast is clear? We don't want to cause any problems. We just want to get back to our own ship."

The girl curled her lip. "Are you asking me to hide you?"

"Yeah, I guess I am." Henry shrugged. "What's your name, anyway?"

"Ruby," the girl said, her eyes narrowed. The tiny gray kitten leaped onto her shoulder, where it perched like a parrot. "Ruby the Brave. And this is Pete the Mighty." She rubbed Pete's cheek. The kitten had already fallen back to sleep, curled around Ruby's neck.

"Ha!" Henry laughed. "Mighty? *That* little ball of fuzz?"

The girl slipped past him. She reached for the door handle. "Want to make fun of us, huh? Go ahead. I'll just let my crew know where you are."

Wally barked in alarm, "Don't do that! He's sorry. Right, Henry? Aren't you sorry?"

Henry grabbed her arm. "I'm sorry I made fun of your cat's name. Will you still help us?" he said quickly. "In case you were wondering, my name's Henry. Just Henry."

"Well, in case *you* were wondering?" said Ruby. "All the best pirates have two names."

"Oh, yeah? What do you know about pirates?" Henry asked.

"Everything," announced Ruby.

Henry shook his head. "Everything, huh? Not as much as me, I bet."

Ruby glared at Henry. "What are you doing with the puppy pirate ship, anyway? Why would you want to hang around with a pack of scurvy dogs?"

"They're my mates!" Henry snapped. "It's a long story."

"Were you a stowaway?" Ruby asked, petting

her kitten. "Pete the Mighty and I were stowaways together." The tiny gray kitten purred in his sleep.

Henry rested his hand on Wally's head. "Well, *we* were even better stowaways."

Ruby and Henry glared at each other.

Puggly rolled her eyes. "Maybe these two should write each other letters and argue about all of this once we get out of here," she grumbled to Wally. "But for now, do you think your human can just focus on getting this lass to help us off this ship?"

"So you want my help, do you, *Just* Henry?" Ruby sighed. "First, I dare you to prove you're a worthy pirate."

"Ask me anything," Henry blurted. "I can prove it."

"Okay," she said, thinking. "Do you know what a ship's kitchen is called?"

Henry laughed. "Are you kidding me? It's

the galley. In case you were wondering, that's simple."

Ruby smirked. "What's another name for a pirate's sword?"

"A cutlass!" Henry said proudly. "Or a nimcha, or a scimitar, or—"

"Okay, okay." Ruby nodded. "Do you know why a lot of human pirates have pierced ears?"

Henry jutted out his chin. "Simple. It's because they think it improves their eyesight."

"Is that true?" Puggly whispered to Wally, pawing at her earrings. "No wonder I can see so well in the dark!"

Ruby narrowed her eyes and grinned. "I've got one more for you. I hope you like riddles. What's a pirate's favorite letter?"

Puggly, Spike, and Wally all exchanged a confused look.

But Henry didn't look at all worried. "*R*. As

in, *arrrrrr*!" He grinned. "But in case you were wondering, that's not a riddle. It's a joke."

"Congratulations. You got them all right," Ruby said. "But if you actually knew anything about pirates, you would know you should never trust your enemy." She flung open the door to her quarters and screamed, "Here, kitty, kitties! The prisoners are in here!"

Cooking Up a Plan

Wally, Spike, Puggly, and Henry dashed through the kitten ship's winding corridors, trying to escape. Hundreds of feet padded behind them. The kittens were closing in. The ship was filled with angry hissing and meowing.

All the twisty hallways and small rooms made it easier for the puppy pirate team to stay ahead of the cats. But after a while, Wally slowed to a walk. "We'll never get off this ship if we keep having to run and hide," he said, panting. "We need a better plan."

Spike whined, "But these are *cats*! Mean, hissing, horrible beasts. We've got to hide, mates. They scare me."

"We have to figure out a smart way to fight back," Wally said.

"There are four of us and a whole ship full of furballs," Puggly noted. "We can't fight. We'd be doomed."

Wally sniffed the air. "Do you smell something strange?"

Puggly snorted. "Yeah, cat puke. Or cat food. They smell the same to me."

"The galley!" Wally yelped. He suddenly remembered something the Claw had said back in the brig. And it gave him an idea. "We have to find the galley."

Before the others could ask questions, Wally

was off. He followed his nose. He sniffed until he found a door that opened into a small, hot room that smelled even *more* like cat than the rest of the ship did.

Spike licked his chops. "Smells kind of yummy. I'm so hungry."

"Looks like we found the galley, mates," Henry whispered. The walls were lined with crates of canned cat food and boxes filled with smoked tuna.

Spike shuddered. "Yuck! Cat food? I can't believe I thought it smelled good in here."

It did kind of smell like Steak-Eye's stew in the kitten ship galley. Wally giggled. He was the only pup on their crew who knew about Steak-Eye's secret ingredient: Kitty Kibble. Wally's tummy growled. It had been hours since their last meal!

"Why did you want to find the galley, Wally?" Puggly asked, poking her nose under a tall table. "Are you thinking they hid Steak-Eye's stolen bag of steaks in here?"

In fact, Wally wasn't thinking about food at all. He was pretty sure the key to his plan was hidden somewhere in this room. "Remember when Fluffy the Claw said no one ever comes in here? That it was a good place to hide things?"

"You think I was listening to that furball?" Puggly said.

Wally sniffed around the edges of the room,

following a strange scent. Finally, he found what he was looking for. A huge cardboard box. "It's here!" he ruffed.

"You found the steaks?" Puggly barked, running over.

Henry peered into the box and gasped. "This is a box of catnip toys!"

"Aye," said Wally. "The Claw hid them here, because he knew what would happen if the crew got their claws on them!" He looked at the others to see if they had caught on.

"Are you thinking what I'm thinking?" Puggly said happily. "Prank time?"

"Well . . . sort of," Wally said.

"*Arr-arr-arooo!*" Puggly woofed.

Wally nudged the box of catnip toys out from under the table. "Remember when the Claw said that if the kitten pirates got ahold of the catnip toys they would all leave their posts? He said there would be chaos on the ship."

"Aye," Puggly snorted.

"We should distract the cats with the catnip!" Henry said, clapping. "Escape while the enemy is playing."

Wally woofed, "Exactly."

Spike looked hopeful. "Maybe this box of toys will keep the cats busy enough that we can finally get out of here."

Henry lifted the box. The four friends hurried through the maze of the kitten ship. Every time they heard kitten claws closing in on them, Henry dropped one of the toys.

The pups heard the kittens mewing with delight and pawing at the toys behind them. The plan was working!

"I smell fresh air!" Wally said, rounding a corner. "Mates—stairs!"

The pups raced each other to the top of a long staircase. They gulped in breaths of salty air. Way over on the starboard side of the ship,

two kitten pirates were swabbing the deck. Other than those two, the coast was clear.

"Yo ho haroo!" howled Spike, running to the deck rail.

"Shhh!" Puggly shushed him. She pointed to the horizon and whispered, "Look over yonder. I see the *Salty Bone!*"

"Our friends are coming to rescue us!" Wally barked.

Puggly put her paws on the rail. She peered over the edge and wagged her curly tail. "There's a dinghy!"

Dangling from the railing at the other end of the boat was a small dinghy, just big enough for a crew of four. "To the dinghy!" urged Henry, running toward it.

"*Meow!*" Before they could reach the escape boat, a hiss sliced through the air. "Kittens, all claws on deck. The puppy pirates are trying to get away!"

Ready Oar Not

"Run!" Spike yowled. "Kitty attack!"

"No more running," Wally said firmly as kitten pirates swarmed the deck. "It's time to show these cats what puppy pirates are made of."

"It is?" Spike asked, trying to hide behind Puggly. But since Puggly was the size of Spike's head, she wasn't a great cover.

"It is," Wally said. He stood tall and proud. "Are you ready to get off this ship?"

"Um, yes?" Spike didn't sound very sure. But he slowly got back on his feet and stood beside Wally.

"We can do this, Spike," Wally said.

Spike was shaking with fear. They were surrounded.

Wally barked at Puggly, "Ready?"

"Fun time!" Puggly yipped. She wound her squat body between Henry's legs, jumped up on her hind legs, and knocked the box out of Henry's hands. The catnip-filled toys fanned out across the deck. "Here, kitty, kitty!"

Every cat on board shrieked. There was a tangle of claws and tails as the kittens fought over the toys. Moopsy and Boopsy batted a toy chili pepper back and forth.

There weren't enough toys for everyone, so the kitten pirates played tug-of-war. In no time, half the toys had been torn open. The air was filled with swirling, whirling flakes of catnip.

Fluffy the Claw pounced on a toy fish. "Stop it!" he hissed at himself. "Stop it, the Claw! You're setting a bad example!" But the catnip was too wonderful for even the first mate to resist.

"Stand guard!" Lucinda the Loud shouted, hissing at her crew for order. But soon the catnip tempted even the captain. She grabbed the toy chili pepper from Moopsy and Boopsy, and her body began to wiggle.

"Kittens!" Ruby the Brave screamed. "The puppy pirates are getting away!"

While the cats played, Henry and the puppy pirates wove a path across the deck, through the catnip-crazy kittens. No one stopped them as they climbed into the dinghy.

Henry began to let the rope out on the dinghy, lowering their escape boat toward the water. In the distance, the *Salty Bone* was cutting through the rough seas.

"Not so fast," Ruby the Brave said, leaning over the deck rail. She put her foot on the rope. The dinghy was stuck. It dangled halfway between the ship's main deck and the sea. Ruby smirked. "You're not going anywhere. Doggies, stay!"

Ruby and Henry stared each other down. Suddenly, Moopsy and Boopsy leaped onto Ruby's head. She shrieked, "What are you cats doing?"

Puggly glanced up. "What *are* they doing?"

Ruby's voice was muffled by two fluffy kitten tails. "Get off me!" she cried. "I can't see anything. The puppy pirates are going to escape."

"You heard her," Moopsy and Boopsy purred at Wally and his friends. "Go. Escape."

"Wait, you're helping us?" Wally asked. "But you're kitten pirates."

"We're helping *you*, pup," the Siamese twins meowed at Wally. "Because you helped us on the dock this morning. You stopped that puggy prank. Cats are nothing if not fair. We always repay our debts."

72

Henry took his chance while Ruby's face was covered in fur. He tugged at the rope again. He lowered their boat the rest of the way to the water. "See you again someday, Ruby the Brave." Henry lifted his hand in a salute as their dinghy floated away from the *Nine Lives*.

Moopsy and Boopsy hopped off Ruby's head. "You can bet on it!" Ruby shouted back at Henry.

The dinghy rocked and rolled on the waves. Henry reached for the oars. But a wave made the boat sway, and he tripped over Spike.

Knocked off balance, Spike tumbled into Puggly.

Puggly knocked against Wally.

And Wally bumped into the oar . . . just hard enough to knock it over the side of the dinghy. The oar splashed into the water.

Henry lunged for it, but the oar slipped out

of his grip. It floated out of reach, bouncing along on the waves.

They were stranded.

"In case you were wondering? You can't row a boat with only one oar," Henry said with a sigh.

"What are we going to do now?" Spike cried. "Bulldogs can't swim! I sink like a stone."

Puggly flopped onto the bottom of the boat. "I can swim a little, but there's no way I would make it all the way to the *Salty Bone*. Me legs are too short."

Wally gulped. He had an idea, but it scared him. "I could try to fetch the oar."

"Well, there you go," Puggly said happily. "You're a retriever. You were born to fetch!"

Wally shivered. He dunked his paw into the water. It was so cold and so, so wet. The sea was gray and huge and scary-looking. Could he do it? "I . . . ," Wally began. He pulled his paw away from the ocean waves. How could he tell his crew he was too scared to save them?

"You don't have to do it if you're afraid," Spike whispered. "I never do anything I'm scared of."

Wally looked at his friend and shook his head. "That's not true, Spike. You've been doing things you're scared of all day."

Spike sniffed. "Only because you told me I could! And because you promised to help me."

"I said you could because I *knew* you could, Spike," said Wally. "You're big, and you're tough. You could do almost anything you wanted if you tried."

"Well, gosh . . . when you put it that way," Spike said, sitting up tall. "I guess I am big and strong. I was born tough, just like you were born to swim."

Watching Spike puff out his chest with

pride made Wally smile. It also made him feel sure. Just because he was afraid didn't mean he couldn't do it. He had swum once. He probably could do it again. "I'm going to get that oar."

Wally took a deep breath. Then he leaped into the freezing-cold ocean.

10

Hair Ball Horror

The water felt like ice on Wally's skin. But it was easier to paddle than he thought it would be. He felt bouncy and light, almost like he was a boat floating on the rolling waves. He breathed through his nose, careful not to open his mouth to let in any of the salty sea water.

With his friends cheering for him in the little dinghy, Wally paddled through the waves. His legs were strong and sure. He reached the oar in no time. He wrapped his mouth around the handle and began to swim back. Again, he was careful not to breathe through his mouth. This was harder to do now that he was towing something.

"You can do it, mate!" Henry screamed. "Fetch, boy."

"Our hero," barked Spike.

"Yo ho ho, mighty pirate," arfed Puggly.

Wally's legs were growing tired. But he was almost there.

"Got it!" Henry shouted, reaching into the water to grab the oar out of Wally's mouth.

As Henry settled back into the boat, Spike reached his mouth over the side and pulled Wally out of the water by the scruff of his neck. "You okay?" he asked.

Wally shook off. "Yes," he barked. And he was. He was more than okay. Because this time, swimming hadn't left him shaky and scared. This time, he came out of the water feeling like a hero. He had done it!

Henry sat on a small bench in the center of the boat. He pulled the oars through the water. But as they began to move toward the *Salty Bone,* something flew through the air at the dinghy. It landed in the water. *Plop.*

Another. *Plip.*

Another. *Plunk.*

Spike screeched and hid under Henry's legs. "The kittens are shootin' cannonballs at us. Row faster." He clawed at Henry's legs.

Plip. Plop. Splash.

"What in the . . . ?" Puggly ruffed. "Those aren't cannonballs! They're throwin' *hair balls.*" She giggled. "That is disgusting . . . and clever."

Wally barked, urging Henry to go faster.

The kittens launched hair ball after hair ball. Whenever one landed in the boat, Spike yelped and swatted it back out.

Soon they were far enough from the kitten ship that the hair balls couldn't reach them anymore. Ahead, they could see their friends on the main deck of the *Salty Bone*.

Curly was at the top of the crow's nest. Her tiny voice rang out loud and clear, "Ahoy, mateys!"

The whole crew worked together to pull the dinghy out of the water. The four friends tumbled out of their tiny boat and onto the deck of the *Salty Bone*. The rest of the puppy pirates surrounded them, barking a welcome.

"It's great to be home!" Wally said.

Piggly ran over to greet her sister. The two pugs wrestled and giggled as Puggly told Piggly all about their adventures on the *Nine Lives*.

Steak-Eye trotted over to the pug twins. "Where are me steaks?" he growled at Puggly.

She eyed him but said nothing.

Steak-Eye snapped, "Lost 'em, eh?"

Piggly and Puggly waited for the cook to explode with anger.

Instead, Steak-Eye laughed. "Guess that means I'll have eight extra paws in the kitchen for the next few weeks. Piggly and Puggly, report for duty in the galley tomorrow morning before the sun comes up."

Puggly groaned. But Piggly grinned. "Fine with me. Kitchen duty means more snacks!"

"In case you were wondering?" Henry told the rest of the crew. "You've got to be one tough pirate to escape a catnapping!"

Spike nodded. "A mighty tough pirate." He yawned, then tucked his tail between his legs. "And this tough guy is headed to bed. I'm going to curl up for a nice, long nap. Bravery is tiring!" He slipped away.

Captain Red Beard growled, "We need to figure out how to get revenge on those frisky cats."

Piggly and Puggly cheered.

"Revenge!" Puggly shouted. "I've got lots of ideas for you, Captain."

Old Salt stepped forward. "Consider your next step carefully, Captain."

"Why?" Red Beard said, looking down at his feet. "Am I going to step in something sticky?"

"I just mean, maybe it's best to end this here," said Old Salt. "Don't go looking for more trouble."

Wally nodded. As much as he loved battles and adventures, the only thing he wanted now was a little nap. He had spent enough time with the kitten pirates to last him for a good, long while. He yawned, then curled up beside Henry. On the horizon, they could see the kitten ship sailing into the setting sun.

Captain Red Beard howled, "Don't go

lookin' for trouble?" Then he grumbled, "But I'm a pirate. Trouble is my middle name."

"Then let's set sail for our next adventure," Old Salt said with a smile. "We can wait for trouble to find us. It always does."

About the Author

Erin Soderberg lives in Minneapolis, Minnesota, with her husband, three adventure-loving kids, and a mischievous goldendoodle named Wally. Before becoming an author, she was a children's book editor and a cookie inventor, and she also worked for Nickelodeon. She has written many books for young readers, including the Quirks series. Erin writes the Puppy Pirates series for her own kids, who love to read and are a big help when it comes to writing the funny stuff.